GOOD KNIGHT ✤ BAD KNIGHT
and the
FLYING MACHINE

Tom Knight

templar
books

D0191935

PROLOGUE

"**P**ass me that last bit of cheese, would you?" said the big, hairy barbarian.

Boog was staring at the last morsels on the cheese board hungrily. His companion, Oog, stabbed a piece of Cheddar with a rusty dagger and passed it over.

"You'll have nightmares, boss," he said.

Boog stuffed the stinky square into his big,

tangled beard, and tried to find his mouth.

"But I LIKE nightmares," Boog said. "It's where I get all my best ideas."

He yawned, and scratched his back with his club. He'd stuck bits of metal into it so that it would give him a really good itching through his thick back hair.

Oog took a big slurp of milk and wiped his moustache with the back of a dirty hand.

"Where are your manners?" said Boog.

"You should stick out your pinky when you drink milk, like this."

Boog stuck out his little finger, and slurped the last of his milk from his wooden goblet.

"We gotta maintain standards, Oog," he said, milk dripping from his moustache. "I mean, look at this lot. They're a shambles."

There were snoring barbarians everywhere. They were covered in cheese crumbs and rats were scurrying all over them, nibbling

up the leftovers. Boog picked up the nearest
rat by its tail and glared at it.

"No wonder we've got a plague problem.
This place is filthy! There's not even
a proper place to have a wash. I had
to scrub my armpits with a damp fish
this morning."

He dropped the terrified rat, which
scarpered off into a bush to have a lie down.

"It's like we're living in the Dark Ages
or something. It's embarrassing! People

will look back on these times and think we're barbarians."

"But we ARE barbarians!" said Oog.

"Not for much longer," said Boog, grinning. "See, I've been doin' a spot of reading . . ."

Boog pulled out a tattered book. Oog was astonished. He'd had no idea that Boog could read.

"It's all about being classy and how to have a bit of decorum. Look . . ."

Civilisation for peasants
Sir Dane le Pompousse

Boog held the book up. It was called *Civilisation for Peasants*[1].

"Erm, that's very nice, boss, but we've got bigger problems. That was the last of our cheese, and the milk barrels are all empty. We're going to have to do another raid on the village."

Boog twirled his moustache thoughtfully.

"All right, but we're not gonna do it the usual way, with all the shouting and screaming and pillaging and stuff. We're gonna be civilised from now on."

Oog looked at his chief as if he'd gone mad.

"Um, what have you got in mind?" he asked nervously.

"We're gonna open a Bank of Milk," grinned Boog, showing broken teeth. "We're

9

* Go to page 174 to look up any words with a number beside them.

not going to be barbarians any more, oh no. We're going respectable. We're gonna be bankers!"

Later that night in the village, a woman with golden hair watched the barbarians advance down the mountainside in a cloud of dust. She quickly scribbled a note and tied it to the leg of her trusted pigeon. "Find him as quickly as you can, Hermes. They're coming!"

With that, she launched the bird out of the window, and watched it disappear into the night sky.

1.

DIY

Warrick and Berk stared into the huge barrel of poo.

"You know, Warrick, this wasn't the fun summer I had in mind," sighed Berk.

"I know," said Warrick. "I mean, it's great that your family are helping us to fix up Pitchkettle Cottage, but this is a job for a hoddypeak[2]."

"How's that daub[3] coming

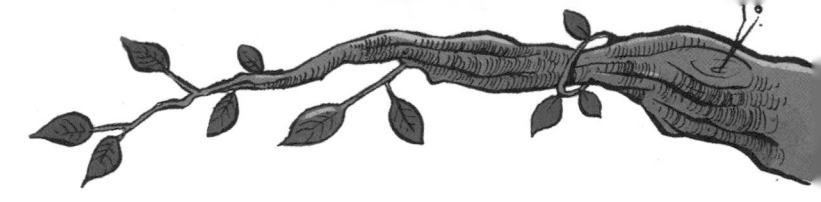

along?" shouted Isobel, Berk's mum. She and Patience, Berk's sister, were sitting on two huge horses that were pulling oak beams through a series of ropes and pulleys up to the roof.

Patience looked at her brother, winking smugly. "Stirry stirry, Berky-Werky!"

"How come SHE gets to sit on a horse all day and we're stirring barrels of poo?" complained Berk.

Warrick winked. "Don't worry, I've got a plan . . ."

He pulled two small vials from his

robes, which he emptied into the barrel:

Drool of centaur, hair of elf,
help this doo-doo stir itself.

The mess inside began to bubble and swirl.

"It's working!" hissed Warrick. "Start adding the straw and clay."

They began shovelling the mixture into the barrel, and looked in wonder as the daub began to form.

At the other end of the cottage Berk's cousin, Godwin, had a feeling something funny was going on. He put down the axe that he had been using to make shingles for the roof, and beckoned to Willow, Warrick's twin sister.

"What are those two up to?" he whispered.

They crept closer, and saw the self-stirring daub, and the delighted, goofy looks on Berk and Warrick's faces.

"Oh no!" Willow said. "They're using magic! Mum'll kill them . . ."

Berk and Warrick stopped shovelling and grinned at each other. "This is so much easier than doing it by hand!" said Warrick. Berk began to look troubled. "Is it me, or is it stirring itself a bit too quickly?"

The gloop was bubbling, and some of it was splashing over the sides. Berk began to panic. "Warrick, slow it down!"

"I don't think I can!"

The barrel started to shake, and some of its

contents spilled over the brim. Soon, it was whirling so fast that the mixture rose out of the barrel like some sort of poo tornado.

"Warrick! Do something!" cried Berk.

Suddenly the barrel burst, flinging a mess of clay, straw and poo EVERYWHERE.

Berk and Warrick were thrown to the

BOOM!

ground. They got up slowly, blinking at the destruction around them. Everything was covered in poo.

"Warrick PITCHKETTLE!" came an angry voice. Hildred, Warrick's mum, was striding across the lawn. Her husband Wenlock came running behind.

WHAT HAVE I TOLD YOU ABOUT USING MAGIC? THIS IS EXACTLY WHY! LOOK AT THE STATE OF THIS PLACE!

"You should know better too, Berkley Paggle," said Isobel. "You'll both need to spend the rest of the weekend clearing this place up."

"AND NO MAGIC!" added Hildred. She turned to her husband. "Cast a hex spell, Wen. Warrick and Willow can do

their chores without magic for a while."

Willow protested. "But Mum . . . !"

"That's enough, Willow. I know you've been using spells to tame our chickens."

Wenlock blinked at his wife. He had once been a great warlock and battled many powerful foes, but he knew better than to argue with Hildred. Raising his hands above his head, he began to chant.

Blue lightning seeped from his fingertips and formed two tangled crowns of smoke around Willow and Warrick's heads. Then it disappeared into the air with a hiss.

Isobel thrust a mop into Berk's hands. "Now get scrubbing – the sun will be down in a couple of hours."

Godwin produced his lute. "Mayhaps we need a little song to hasten our labours!"

Oooooohh Hubert hauled a heavy hoe, dum-dilly-dilly—

SPLAT! A lump of horse poo hit Godwin square on the forehead.

2.

SAD SUMMER DAYS

Berk was sitting in the crooked branch of a sycamore tree, swinging his feet angrily and dropping bits of bark onto Warrick's head.

"Stop it Berk!" Warrick shouted. "It wasn't MY fault the spell went wrong!"

"Yeah, but it was your idea to use magic. We've just wasted two days cleaning up. I wish we were at the bladderball summer camp with Jax and the others."

Jax Rutterkin was the coolest kid in school, and last term he'd wanted to hang out with Berk because Berk had defeated a dragon with a catapult and a troll-breath stink bomb. Jax and his friends had even asked him to join the school bladderball team.

Berk found that being cool was pretty exhausting, but it was nice being popular for a change. But then Warrick had accidentally transported them all to another dimension, where they'd had to battle an evil horde, shut a magic portal and rescue Warrick's dad and sister.

All that magic had seemed a bit much for Jax and the others, so they had jumped at the chance to go to the relative safety of bladderball camp for the whole summer.

Berk wasn't sure he missed chucking balls around and falling in mud, but surely it would have been better than cleaning up poo.

Willow was lying on her back in the long grass, watching two dragonflies zigzagging

through the air above her head.

"I can't BELIEVE you got us hexed!" she said to her brother. "Mum would never have figured out I'd been using magic to tame the chickens if it wasn't for you!"

Godwin was ignoring all of them. He had been doing a series of exhausting looking exercises for the last hour.

"You lot . . . pff . . . really should . . . pff . . . concentrate on . . . pfft . . . brushing up on . . . pff . . . your knight skills . . . pff!" he panted, whilst doing star jumps. "School starts . . . oofftt . . . in a week . . . pfft!"

"Urgh, don't remind me!" said Berk.

Godwin dropped to the ground and began doing press-ups.

"Besides, Sir Dane le Pompousse . . . pff . . . says that being fit is one of the main building blocks of a civilised society . . . oofftt . . . as well as having a positive attitude and terrific hair."

"Yeah, but Sir Dane is a complete hoddypeak, so what would he know?" said Berk.

Godwin had become obsessed with a book called *Civilisation for Peasants* by Sir Dane le Pompousse. It was full of tips on how to act chivalrously and how to have proper manners. Berk had only managed to read a few pages before throwing it down

the well in disgust. Godwin had to climb down with a rope to fish it out, and didn't speak to Berk for days afterwards. He now kept the book with him wherever he went.

Warrick was turning a small sycamore seed round in his fingers and making notes in his book. The seeds had little wings, and he had been watching them spin through the air as they fell from the tree.

"Zooks, imagine if we made a really big version of these seeds and hung a seat underneath! We could fly!"

Berk wasn't convinced. "Yeah, but these only go down. We'd want to go UP."

"You're right," said Warrick. He looked dreamily at the clouds. "I could use a spell to fly if we hadn't been hexed."

"I've got a book at home that might help," said Berk. "Mum bought it for me when I was building my catapult. It's by some weird looking inventor bloke, but it's all in Italian so I never read it. I'm sure it has some drawings of machines that can fly. You can have it if you want."

Warrick sat up straight. "Yes please! Zooks, imagine if we had our own flying machine!"

Berk imagined hundreds of winged machines zooming over

a battlefield, releasing fizzing stink bombs onto the enemy below.

"We could sell whole fleets of them to whoever had the most gold. We'd be RICH!"

Godwin looked at his cousin with disapproval. "Where's your sense of chivalry, Berk? Knights are meant to help people!"

Willow sat up. "But just think how

many people we could help. We'd have the roof on Pitchkettle Cottage in no time!"

"Well, I just want to get famous for something other than swinging a silly sword around," said Warrick. "And I won't get rich and famous with magic if I can't practise my spells any more."

"You certainly need the practice!" snorted Willow. "Otherwise you'll be famous for being the only wizard in the world who covers everything in poo."

Willow was interrupted by a chaotic flapping sound. A chicken was

careering through the air towards them. Finally it crash-landed at Willow's feet. She scooped it up into her arms where it clucked happily.

"This is one of the hens from Pitchkettle Cottage," she said. "She must have really missed me!"

Warrick started furiously scribbling in his notebook. "You know, watching that chicken's flight path has given me an idea . . ."

3.

BUMPTON HILL

Strap them on nice and tight!" shouted Berk. He was eagerly clutching the lever of his catapult, while Warrick and Willow strapped some big leaves to Godwin's arms. Godwin was sitting in the catapult's bowl, looking nervous.

"Are you sure this will work?" he asked Warrick.

"I think so!" said Warrick. "I was up all night looking at that book of Berk's and the pictures gave me some great ideas. I just wish I could read Italian."

"I'm not sure this is a good idea," said Willow, pulling a strap tight.

"He'll be fine," said Warrick. "You just have to remember to flap, Godwin."

"Speaking of flapping, why have you brought that chicken with you, Willow?" asked Berk.

The chicken from yesterday was sitting at Willow's feet.

"You mean Lettuce?" said Willow. "She's been following me everywhere. I think she thinks I'm her mum."

WAAAAAHHH!

Godwin looked very nervous.

"Can you please stop talking about chickens and just concentrate on . . . WAAAAAAAAAAAAAAAAAHHH!"

Berk had pulled the lever. Godwin was launched straight through the air, his wings torn off with the force of the acceleration. He disappeared into some trees and Berk, Willow and Warrick heard branches snapping, and then a faint SPLOSH. Warrick and Willow ran down the hill to help, while Berk rolled on his back, tears of laughter streaming down his cheeks.

35

He was still laughing when they came trudging back up the hill. Godwin was covered in pond mud.

"You were meant to FLAP!" squealed Berk.

A frog hopped out of Godwin's boot, looking confused.

"I need to make some more studies," said Warrick. "There were all sorts of bird drawings in Berk's book. Maybe we need to look at something that's better at flying than a chicken."

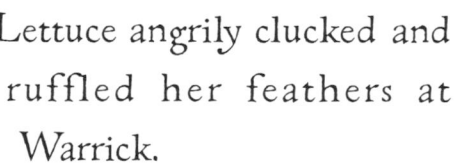

Lettuce angrily clucked and ruffled her feathers at Warrick.

"I know where we need to go," said Willow.

She pointed to a jagged mountain in the distance,

where they could just see the shapes of eagles circling the misty peak.

"The Snaggletooth Mountain?" spluttered Berk. "Are you crazy? My dad says it's full of trolls and bandits!"

"Are you a knight or a chicken?" said Willow, and they all danced around Berk waggling their elbows up and down and clucking. Lettuce looked at them like they had all gone mad.

4.

FOUR GO CAMPING

"hi-hoooooo!"

Berk glowered as he watched Godwin spring over rocks and boulders.

"Why do you keep 'hi-hooooing'? You sound like an absolute fopdoodle[4]," he grumbled.

"Well, someone has the mubblefubbles[5] today!" said Godwin cheerfully.

"Just get a lungful of that fresh air!"

The four friends had been walking all afternoon, and had just reached the foothills of the mountain.

"Do you think our parents believed our story about camping by the river?" said Warrick.

"I don't know why we couldn't tell them the truth," said Godwin. "Sir Dane says, 'A true knight must hold the truth as tenderly as he would hold the hand of a beautiful maiden.'"

Willow snorted. "Why would anyone want *him* holding their hand?" She looked around. "Let's camp here for the night." As she set down her satchel, Lettuce popped her head out of the top. "Out you come," said Willow, and the chicken flapped up to her shoulder.

Godwin and Warrick went to collect some firewood, while Willow and Berk put up the tent. Before long, they had built themselves quite a cosy camp.

"Right, how are we going to light this fire?" said Berk.

"Leave that to me!" said Warrick.

He took off his glasses and angled them to catch the sunlight. Soon the pine needles started to smoke and Warrick blew on them until a flame appeared.

"Woah, how did you do that?" said Berk, impressed.

"I dunno!" said Warrick. "I think my glasses make the sunlight stronger or something. I've been discovering all sorts of things since I stopped relying on magic!"

Soon the sun disappeared behind the mountain.

"I'm glad we've got this fire going," said Willow. "It's freezing!"

"Never mind the cold," said Warrick. "What's that horrid smell?"

They had all noticed the stink.

"I reckon it's Godwin!" said Berk.
"All those exercises he's been doing have
been playing havoc with his insides!"

"It's not coming from me!" protested
Godwin. "I think it's coming from up
there . . ."

He pointed up the dark mountain.
Somewhere an eagle screeched, and a
wolf howled in reply.

Willow shivered. "Brrrr, sing us

a happy song, Godwin! Did you bring your lute?"

Godwin shook his head. "No – I couldn't find it this morning."

Everyone looked at Berk, who pulled his best innocent face.

"I could tell you a story instead, but it's not a very happy one, I'm afraid." Godwin stirred the fire with a stick, and began to tell his tale.

"Have I ever told you why I came to live here?"

"Yeah," said Berk. "Your mum and dad are farmers and they sent you to learn how to be a knight from my mum and dad."

"Yes, that's part of it, but it's not the whole story. My village is a long way north, nearly as far as you can go. My mum and dad have got hundreds of cows. They've lived off milk and cheese for generations up there."

"Speaking of cheese, have you let one off again?" interrupted Berk, wafting his hand in front of his face.

Willow threw a pebble at Berk to shut him up. Godwin continued.

"Everything was fine until a couple of years ago. One day, a horde of barbarians came down from the mountains. They wanted our milk, and said they would come back every month for more. Now my parents have to work twice as hard. It's wearing them out!

"I wanted to stay and protect the village, but my father said I had to go away to learn how to be a knight. I didn't want to go at first, but your family have been so kind to me."

Godwin looked over at his cousin who, for once, stayed quiet.

"I can't stop thinking about Mum and Dad though, and those horrible barbarians. Someone has to teach them a lesson, and I'm not sure I can wait until I become a knight. If we had a flying machine we could just whizz over and scare the barbarians off."

For a while, the four friends were quiet as they stared into the fire.

"Well, we'd better get some sleep," said Warrick, clapping his hands. "We've got eagles to study in the morning!"

5.

THE CAVE OF STINK

Pooh, it's gedding worse!" said Berk. They were getting nearer to the top of the mountain, and the smell was so bad they'd stuffed moss up their nostrils.

Soon, they reached the mountaintop. Several gnarled trees trembled in the wind, which howled round the entrance of a large cave.

"Look, over dere!" whispered Warrick.

Two magnificent eagles were perched on a branch next to a large nest. Nearby were several eaglets, stretching their wings and hopping from rock to rock.

"Dey're pracdising flying! Dis is perfecd!" hissed Warrick. He pulled out his sketchbook and a piece of charcoal and began furiously scribbling.

"Dey're so beaudiful!" said Willow – she looked completely enchanted.

Berk frowned. "Dey look bicious to me!"

"Berks wight," said Warrick. "We bedder be careful. De big ones won't like us being anywhere near de eaglets."

That was all Berk needed to hear. "Can we please ged oud of here and study dem frob a bit furder away?"

But Willow had left their hiding place

behind the rock, and was walking over
to the nest for a better view. Warrick,
Godwin and Berk began hissing at her to
come back, but she seemed to be in some
sort of trance. Suddenly, Lettuce poked
her head out Willow's bag, spotted an
eagle, and started clucking furiously. With
a screech, both the eagles leapt off the
branch and began circling in the air above
Willow's head.

Godwin ran into the clearing with both
his hands held out.

"Fear nod brave eagles!" he cried.

"We bean you no harmb!"

Godwin's voice seemed to snap Willow out of her trance, and she looked up just in time to see an eagle swooping at her head. Before she could move, Godwin dived towards her, knocking her out of

its path. Lying on their backs in a cloud of dust, they looked up to see the second eagle coming right for them.

"Oh, Zooks[6]!" cried Warrick. He jumped onto a rock and began to cast a spell:

Oh mountain rock, gib me de strength
to keep dat eagle at arm's length.

"Warrick you ninny, you forgod about de hex!" yelled Berk.

There was a honking sound, and

the blue-smoke crown appeared around Warrick's head, causing him to stagger and fall off the rock.

Godwin and Willow lay flat on the ground, expecting the eagle to attack at any moment. But just then, a deafening roar echoed from the mouth of the cave.

Startled, the eagles retreated to their nest. The mountaintop shook with heavy footsteps and a huge black shape appeared in the mouth of the cave. Even with the moss in their nostrils, the stench became unbearable. Willow and Godwin scrambled

back behind the rock – just in time to see
an enormous dragon step into the sunlight.

Berk felt his legs turn to jelly.
"Run for it!" he screamed.

6.

SAFE HOUSE

Berk, Godwin, Warrick and Willow sat around Berk's kitchen table. A huge fire roared in the hearth, and Isobel was ladling a steaming milk and honey mixture into bowls.

"This will warm you up," she said. "Who would have thought that camping by the river would be so traumatic – you're shaking, Berk!"

"Yes, he is isn't he?" said Patience, who had just wandered into the kitchen. "Did widdle Berkley-Werkely miss his teddy bear?"

Isobel swept Patience out of the room before Berk could reply. "We're just off to check on the horses – help yourself to more milk."

As soon she had shut the heavy wooden door behind her, Berk began burbling. "I'm telling you, it was HIM!" he said. "The dragon I defeated with the troll-breath stink bomb!"

"It certainly explains where the smell was coming from," said Godwin. "I told you it wasn't anything to do with me."

"That poor creature!" said Willow. "I think the stink has made him ill. No wonder he was so angry."

Godwin adopted a heroic pose, just like Sir Dane on the cover of *Civilisation for Peasants*. "There's only one thing to do. We must slay it!"

Willow immediately jumped up, knocking her bowl of milk into Berk's lap.

"Don't you DARE!" she hissed. "If you go anywhere NEAR that dragon with your stupid sword, you'll regret it!"

Godwin gulped. He'd seen the

sort of spells Willow was capable of, and he didn't want to risk her anger, hexed or not.

"Calm down you two!" said Warrick. "We've got better things to do than dragon slaying!"

Warrick took out the book by the Italian inventor that Berk had given him. "I've figured something out after seeing those eagles. Look at these pictures . . ."

Everyone peered at the drawings in the book, which were heavily annotated with strange writing. Some of them seemed to show hollow reeds.

"It must be to do with the bones. Look, I found these on the mountain by the cave." He pulled some yellowing bones from his robes.

"Yuck!" said Godwin.

"This is from an eagle's wing," said Warrick. "They're hollow! That's how they can fly."

Lettuce jumped onto the table and began strutting up and down, flexing her wings.

"See!" said Warrick, pointing at the underside of Lettuce's wing. "Look at the way

the feathers are arranged. I reckon all we need is some hollow reeds from the riverbank, and as many feathers as we can get our hands on."

"But where are we going to get that many feathers?" said Godwin.

"I've got an idea," said Berk. "Who do we know round here who has more chickens than he knows what to do with?"

Godwin snapped his fingers. "Farmer Stuffcock!"

Willow joined in. "Of course. From the other side of Bumpton Hill! He's got those poor chickens squished up in his barn so tight they can barely move."

Berk grinned. "I don't think he'll miss a few feathers, do you? We're going on a chicken run."

7.

THE CHICKEN MISSION

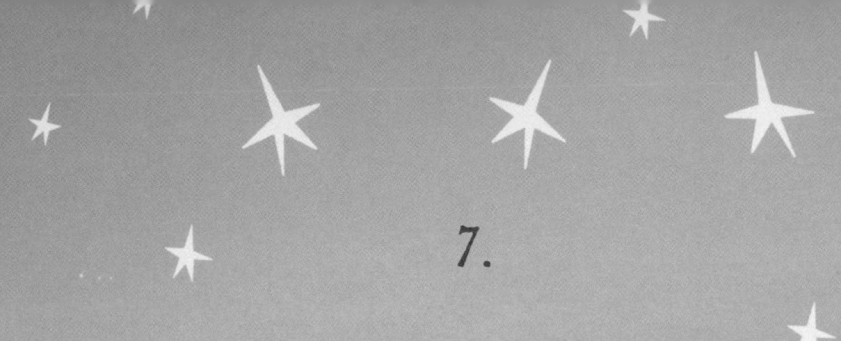It was a moonless night, and the four figures scuttling alongside the hedgerow were barely visible in the gloom.

"I don't agree with all this sneaking. It's unknightly," said Godwin loudly. "Sir Dane says . . . "

"Sssshhh!" hissed Berk, Willow and Warrick at the same time.

Suddenly Berk stopped,

causing everyone to bump into each other in the darkness. Lettuce squawked .

"Careful of the pump!" hissed Warrick. The pump was a long hose attached to a sack, which had a pair of bellows fitted to it. Warrick and Berk had spent the whole afternoon making it.

Berk's plan was simple. They would slip the hose under the barn door and pump the bellows, which would suck all the loose feathers into the sack. Farmer Stuffcock or the chickens would never even know they had been there.

"I still don't think this is the right thing to do. It feels like stealing," complained Godwin.

"It's not stealing!" said Berk. "It's more like sneaky tidying up. Besides, don't you ever get tired of doing the right thing?"

"Not really," said Godwin. "And why did we have to put this blue stuff on our faces?"

"It's not 'blue stuff'," said Willow. "It's woad[7] and warriors paint their faces with it before battle."

"Oh stop moaning, Godwin!" said Berk. "Does everyone remember their emergency signals? Let's practise."

Willow hooted like an owl, Berk howled like a wolf and Warrick ribbited like a frog. Even Lettuce clucked like a chicken. Everyone looked at Godwin who didn't look very happy at all.

"Godwin . . . ?" said Berk, grinning.

Reluctantly, Godwin oinked like a pig.

"Okay, let's move out!" said Berk, pumping his fist in the air.

Crouching low, they ran silently across the field.

When they reached the barn, Berk and Godwin began feeding the pump through the gap under the door.

"Let me know when you're in position," whispered Warrick.

The unhappy clucking from inside the barn was very loud, and Willow peered through a crack in the door. Inside was row upon row of scraggly, miserable looking chickens.

"Those poor creatures!" she wailed. Lettuce wailed too, and started angrily flapping her wings.

"Ssshh, Willow!" said Berk. "Warrick, the pump is in position. Commence sucking!"

Warrick began pumping the bellows, and the sack began to inflate.

"It's working!" cried Berk. "Keep going!"

The three boys were so focussed on the expanding sack that they didn't notice Willow struggling with the heavy wooden beam that kept the door shut.

Finally she pulled the barn door open with a CLUNK.

"Willow! What are you doing?" hissed Berk.

But Willow ignored him, and ran into the barn waving her arms.

The chickens flew into a frenzy as she ran up and down, shooing them from their cramped shelves and yelling, "FREEDOM!" at the top of her voice. Lettuce was following Willow, bouncing up and down and waving her wings.

"Zooks, she's lost her marbles! Pump harder Warrick!"

Suddenly there was a shout. Godwin crept round the back of the barn to investigate and then ran back, oinking wildly and pointing over his shoulder.

"F-farmer S-Stuffcock!" he spluttered. A fat, red-faced man appeared behind him, out of breath from running.

He looked at the three boys with blue faces, the long hose of the pump and

the open barn door. He began to say something, but was knocked off his feet as hundreds of clucking chickens burst out of the barn, flapping their wings. They were followed by a wild, red-haired girl with blue stripes on her cheeks.

"Leg it!" yelled Willow, and the four warriors (and one chicken) disappeared into the darkness.

8.

BACK TO SCHOOL

PAAAARRAARRPP!

Sir Donnick Remarque blew a long blast on his bugle, and looked across the school hall with small, cold eyes. Berk loathed Sir Donnick Remarque, and the feeling was mutual.

"Now children," drawled Sir Donnick. "I have some unfortunate news. Our beloved

Lord de Beef befell a most grievous fate this summer."

Everyone in the hall gasped.

"His past deeds as a knight have finally caught up with him, and I regret to inform you that one of his enemies has turned him into a newt."

The hall erupted into sounds of dismay. All the pupils loved Lord de Beef, and the prospect of a whole term without his cheerful bearded face was terrible.

PAAAAAAAAAAAAARRAAARRRRP!

The chatter was silenced by another bugle blast.

"REST ASSURED we are doing all we can to restore him to his former glory. A team of apothecaries[8] are working round the clock to reverse the spell – so far they have only brought back his eyebrows, but they assure me that he will be fully restored by winter."

"I am happy to tell you, however, that Lord de Beef has left the running of the school in the most capable hands of his nephew. Prithee[9] welcome our temporary head, Sir Dane le Pompousse."

Godwin squeaked like a mouse as the muscular figure swaggered

onto the stage. Berk looked disgusted. "That fopdoodle is Lord de Beef's nephew?"

Godwin seemed to have lost the ability to talk, and just squeaked again.

Sir Dane struck a heroic pose and clicked his fingers. Suddenly several tapestries unfurled at the back of the hall, showing him in

extravagant costumes. Sir Donnick blew a fanfare on his bugle, and Sir Dane began to speak.

"Now young fauntkins[10] settle down. I'm sure you all know me from my bestselling book, *Civilisation for Peasants*.

"It grieves my heart to say that we are living in unenlightened times. Ever since this country was abandoned by the greatest civilisation the world has ever seen, we have been in tatters. I am talking, of course, about the Romans. All of the wondrous roads, cities and banks that they built have been left to crumble, and the country is once again in the hands of barbarians, thieves and smelly old peasants.

"I am therefore proud to be re-civilising this great land – starting with you children."

He waved a finger in the air, and Berk made a gagging sound.

"It is my great privilege to guide you on your paths to becoming knights. In the noble spirit of chivalry however, I must be honest. Some of you will not have the purity of heart or excellent bone structure needed to be truly great. I can already see that many of you lack the basic physical traits that only the truly civilised possess."

Berk was convinced that Sir Dane looked

straight at him and Warrick when he said this.

"The rest of you will pursue the lesser paths – blacksmiths, millers, hedge trimmers, privy[11] scrubbers – and it will be your job to make the kingdom a nicer place for knights and noblemen like us."

Godwin laughed loudly and nervously, and the whole school turned to stare at him.

Sir Dane beamed at Godwin. "Now, off to your lessons. And remember – the path to being truly civilised begins in the heart, but we must not forget to look after our muscles and our hair. Civilisation has no room for ugly people. DISMISSED!"

As everyone shuffled out of the great hall, Berk took one look at Godwin who was wandering in a star-struck daze.

"This is going to be the worst term ever," he said to Warrick.

"No it's not," said Warrick. "We're going to invent a flying machine and become rich and famous."

"Yeah!" said Berk. "Then Sir Dane can scrub OUR privies."

9.

BUNGEE!

Godwin peered over the edge of the battlements and gulped.

"Are you SURE this is going to work?"

Berk and Warrick had spent the weekend building two large wings from the feathers they had taken from Farmer

Stuffcock's barn. They had laid them over a frame made from hollowed reeds, and now they were strapped onto Godwin's arms. The four friends were gathered at the top of the highest tower in Berk's castle for the new wings' first flight.

Several of the chickens from Farmer Stuffcock's barn had taken roost in the tower, and were lined up along the battlements watching the proceedings.

"Just flap as hard as you can and you'll be soaring above the trees in no time," said Warrick.

"Yeah, and if something goes wrong – but it won't – this will save you from getting a dunking in the moat," said Berk.

He was trying a long stretchy cord to Godwin's ankle, which they had made

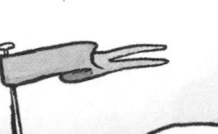

from the horrid sheep intestines that Gregory, Berk's dad, used to make sausages.

Lettuce clucked nervously, and Willow looked as worried as Godwin. "If we are so sure that Godwin will be able to fly, why don't we start on the ground?"

"Where's the fun in that?" asked Berk. "Besides, he'll need the height to get his flap on. Ready?"

Before Godwin could say anything, Berk gave him a gentle shove.

"WAAAAAAAAHHHHH!"

Berk, Warrick, Willow and several chickens peered over the edge of the battlements. Godwin was hurtling towards the ground, flapping desperately.

"You know, I might have made that cord too long," said Berk.

There was a huge SPLASH as Godwin plunged into the moat. Then the cord went tight, and he was yanked out of the

water and pinged back up into the air.

He appeared at the battlement, seemed to hover, and then hurtled back towards the moat.

"FLAP HARDER THIS TIME!" shouted Berk.

"What's the point?" said Warrick sadly. "It's just another failure." He stomped off down the spiral staircase.

"Don't give up!" said Berk, and he chased after Warrick, saying something about automatic flapping mechanisms.

"Boys!" said Willow, shaking her head, and she rushed to the moat to rescue Godwin from the water.

10.

COW ISLAND

ight, line up you horrid lot and let's have a look at ya!"

Boog was slowly walking down the line of barbarians and inspecting their appearance. They were gathered in the village green,

and the villagers were nearby, cowering together in a huddle.

Boog was wearing a battered top hat made from old tree bark. He'd tried to paint it black with mud. He'd also slicked down his moustache with grease, and had shaped his beard into a point with more mud. He looked horrible.

Oog trotted behind. He was wearing a

monocle that he had made from a stone with a hole in it. It kept falling off, so he'd stuck it onto his face with tree sap.

In fact, all the barbarians had made some sort of effort to smarten up. Several had tried to wash themselves – there were big flesh-coloured streaks across their skin – and others had poked flowers into their leather armour. One had tried to cut his own hair, and his head was a mess of stubble and scabs.

"Lovely job!" said Boog, picking a spider out of one barbarian's beard and absent-mindedly popping it into his mouth. "We all look proper respectable. Apart from you Leslie – you look even worse than usual."

The barbarian who'd given himself a haircut looked at his feet while the rest laughed.

"RIGHT!" Boog clapped his hands and turned to address the villagers.

"Ladies and gentlemen! From now on, we are not barbarians. We're BANKERS, got it?"

The villagers stared at Boog in bewilderment.

Even some of the barbarians were looking confused. Boog waved his battered copy of *Civilisation for Peasants* in the air.

"See, it says in here that them Romans kept all their expensive bits and bobs in posh temples. If someone wanted to borrow some bits and bobs then they had to give more bits and bobs than they had borrowed back in return. That's called interest, see? And that's what bankers do."

He opened the book and flicked to a page. "This bit says that banks are one of the cornerstones of civilised society, and I don't

know about you, but I've had enough of mud and rats."

Boog looked down and noticed that he'd stepped in some horse poo. Tutting, he

cleaned it off his boot with the palm of his hand, then wiped his hand down the front of his fur coat.

"That's what I'm talking about. We're gonna bring a bit of civilisation back to this horrible village," he declared. "A bit of order. You can borrow some of our milk, but you've got to pay us back. With interest.

Which means you all work for us now."

A tall blond man was about to step forward but his wife placed a gentle hand on his arm.

"I've sent Hermes with a message to Godwin to send help," she whispered. "Be patient, Gideon."

The man looked at the barbarians with their huge clubs, swords and axes and remained silent.

Boog turned to his barbarians and pointed a thumb over his shoulder at the huge milk barrels. "Make sure the villagers fill these before the next full moon. And no carrying on like savages! If you feel like setting fire to something, use your words instead. Right, I'm off for a nap. GET MILKING!"

11.

CIVILISATION FOR PEASANTS

Sir Dane's chalk screeched as he underlined the long word he had just written on the blackboard.

"Now, who can tell me what this word means?"

Godwin's hand immediately shot up.

"I can, Sir Dane! It says 'Hierarchy', and it means a system where society is ranked according to status, wealth or influence."

"Very good!" said Sir Dane, and he nodded at Godwin's copy of *Civilisation for Peasants*. "I can see someone has done their homework."

Godwin flushed and looked around at his fellow classmates, who all scowled back at him.

"To be truly civilised we must form a hierarchical society," continued Sir Dane. "Alas, many of you are too stupid to understand what that means, so allow me to demonstrate."

He pointed a long finger at Warrick. "You! Come over here."

Warrick reluctantly shuffled to

the front of the class. Sir Dane then turned to Godwin, and bowed slightly. "Godwin, would you please join us too?"

Godwin went and stood beside Warrick.

"Young Godwin here possesses all of the traits that would put him at the top of society. If you need a maiden rescued or a dragon slayed, he's just the sort of fellow to do it."

He turned to Warrick and curled his lips. "This scruffy item, on the other hand, is what the Romans would have referred to as a plebian[12]. A lack of care for personal grooming shows a lack of respect for society. People like this belong at the bottom of the heap. If we are to flourish in this modern world, we must KNOW OUR PLACE."

Sir Dane then cast a cold eye over Berk, who was drawing in his notebook.

"And what would you say your place is?" Berk didn't look up.

"Berk!" Willow hissed, but it was too late. Sir Dane had whipped the notebook out of Berk's hands. "Let's see what's more important than my lessons," he sneered.

When he saw the drawings, he barked

a harsh laugh. The page was covered in diagrams of flying machines.

"This boy thinks he can build some sort of winged chariot. I can see that he needs to be put in his place. DETENTION!"

From deep inside Willow's bag, Lettuce squawked. Sir Dane glared at Willow.

"Did you have something to say in this boy's defence?"

Willow swallowed and looked up.

"Yes, actually. Berk is very good at

making things. Last term he built a catapult and used it to save the school from a dragon."

Sir Dane snorted. "I can see that you need to be re-educated on your position as well. Perhaps you'll both realise your limits by cleaning out the staff privy. Sir Kitt Trayning, the bladderball coach, has apparently had a dreadful case of the flux[13], and the floor needs a thorough mopping.

"B-but that's not fair!" interrupted Warrick. "She didn't do anything!"

"What a surprise," said Sir Dane. "Another volunteer for mopping duty. Detention for all three of you. The sooner you get used to cleaning up after your superiors the better."

12.

IN THE PRIVY

illow, Warrick and Berk stared in horror at the inside of the staff privy. The rushes on the floor had turned a nasty shade of brown.

"I wish we still had some of that moss from the mountain for our nostrils," said Willow. "It stinks in here."

"I wish Sir Dane had got turned into a newt instead of Lord de Beef, but we can't have everything," said Berk. "Come on, let's get this over and done with."

The three friends began cleaning up the privy in silence. Suddenly Warrick threw his mop down in disgust.

"Maybe Sir Dane is right! Maybe we have been stupid, thinking we could build a flying machine."

"What are you talking about, Warrick?" said Berk. "We're so close!"

"No, we're not!" wailed Warrick. "All our flight attempts have been disasters."

Since Godwin's dunking in the moat a few weeks ago, they had ditched the idea of just building wings, and had made a machine which flapped its wings using a crank and pulleys.

"Berk's automatic flapping system worked a treat," said Willow. "We just need to figure out how to stop the nose pitching into the ground."

Warrick just stared at his reflection in a horrible looking puddle. "What's the

point? We should just accept that all we're good for is mopping up poo."

Suddenly Lettuce, who had been watching them from Willow's bag, leaped onto Warrick's lap and began waggling her bottom in his face.

"Get OFF me, Lettuce!" snapped Warrick. "There's no need to rub it in."

But Lettuce carried

on waggling her tail feathers, and at the same time started rotating her wings.

"Is she dancing?" said Berk.

"No, I think she's trying to tell us something," said Willow.

Warrick stared at the chicken for a long time. Suddenly he leaped to his feet, gathered Lettuce in his arms and cuddled her. He then performed a fast dance around the privy, whirling Lettuce in circles.

Berk looked at Willow and twirled a finger around his head. "They've BOTH gone bonkers!"

But Warrick looked at them with delight. "We need a TAIL! And we need the wings to rotate a bit to give us lift. That way the nose will stop pitching into the ground. Lettuce, you're a GENIUS!"

"Well, what are we waiting for?" said Berk. "Let's get back so we can get started on the changes straight away."

Willow frowned. "Aren't you forgetting something? We've still got all this mess to mop up for Sir Dane."

Berk snapped his fingers. "I've got an idea," he said, and he crept out into the corridor. A minute later he came back with bundles of cloth in his arms.

Willow gasped when she realised what they were.

"Sir Dane's tapestries!"

"Yep! I've had enough of seeing his big stupid face all over the school. Now we can finally put them to good use to mop up this stinking privy."

13.

THE FLYING MACHINE

"He's a horrible bully!" said Willow as she helped the others pull the flying machine to the top of Bumpton Hill.

"Sir Dane is NOT a bully!" snapped Godwin. "I'm sorry he gave you all that

detention, but he's just trying to bring a bit of civilisation back to the country. Anyway, that dragon is a much bigger threat than Sir Dane – Sir Dane only wants to help."

"Don't you touch a scale on that poor dragon's head!" snapped Willow.

"And don't try and change the subject!" said Berk. "Everyone knows you're Sir Dane's pet!"

"Oh can everyone stop brangling[14]!" said Warrick. "We'll show that bully who's at

the bottom of the heap when we're flying above his head. I think the changes we've made are really going to work this time."

It had been a busy few days. School had been awful. Sir Dane had made the whole class scour the castle for his missing tapestries, and it was obvious that he suspected Berk was the main culprit. Berk knew that they would never be found at the bottom of the moat where they had sunk them, but Sir Dane's anger and suspicion had been fairly exhausting.

On top of that, they had all been sneaking out of their houses at night to work on the flying machine in the Pitchkettles' barn. The machine looked incredible – like a great wood-and-canvas bird.

They had added a tail with a rudder

system for steering and created flaps at the front of the wings.

Willow and Godwin had argued most of the time.

"We should at least tell one of the teachers about the dragon," continued Godwin. "Sir Dane says that dragons are part of the old, uncivilised times. It says in *Civilisation for Peasants* that they should become extinct."

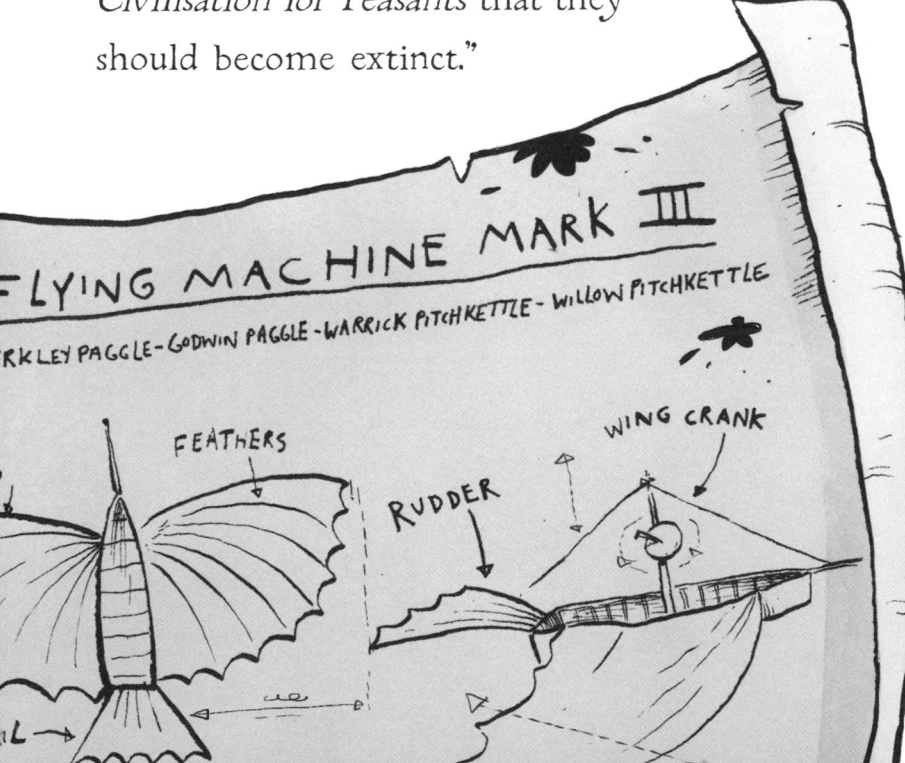

FLYING MACHINE MARK III

RKLEY PAGGLE - GODWIN PAGGLE - WARRICK PITCHKETTLE - WILLOW PITCHKETTLE

FEATHERS

RUDDER

WING CRANK

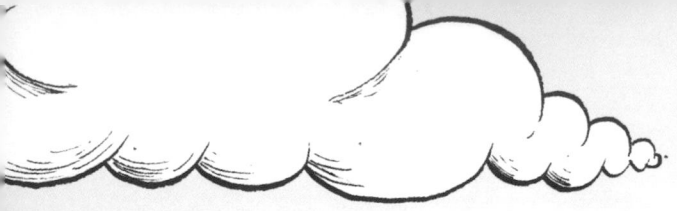

Willow spun around furiously. "I'm going to make you extinct in a minute!"

She had gone bright red.

Godwin could see how upset she was. "Look, Willow, it would be for the dragon's own good if he . . ." but Willow cut him off.

"If you or Sir Dane go anywhere NEAR Snaggletooth Mountain, I'll never speak to you again." And she stormed off down the hill.

"Nice one, cousin," said Berk. "It's usually me that upsets everyone. Maybe we should go after her?"

They had reached the top of Bumpton Hill by now. Willow was a small speck in the distance.

"I'll go after her," said Godwin.

But just at that moment, there was an exhausted cooing sound from above them, and a pigeon burst through the clouds and landed at Godwin's feet.

"Hermes?" he cried.

There was a message tied to the bird's leg. Godwin unrolled the parchment and read quickly, his eyes wild.

"It's my parents – they're in trouble! I have to go and help them. I'm sorry, Warrick, but I need the flying machine!"

Godwin leapt into the cockpit and the

machine began rolling downhill.

Berk cried out in alarm. "Godwin, you've gone bonkers!"

But Godwin was already turning the crank that operated the wings. With a steady *wooomph*, he and the flying machine began to rise into the air.

Warrick grabbed onto one of the dangling ropes. "Come back!"

But Warrick was pulled upwards, feet

thrashing helplessly in the air.

"Come back!" shouted Berk, but before he knew it, he'd jumped up and grabbed onto the rope too.

Far below, Patience was coming home from a horse ride when she saw a flying machine flapping chaotically across the sky. Godwin was in the cockpit and Warrick and Berk dangled below, screaming.

14.

BACK TO THE MOUNTAINS

Willow stared into the night sky, and shivered. She had been furious when she left Bumpton Hill, but now she wished Berk, Warrick and Godwin were with her. She was nearly at the top of Snaggletooth Mountain, and it was cold, dark and very smelly.

She whispered into her satchel, "At least

I've got you for company, Lettuce."

The chicken gave an uncertain cluck. She was shivering too.

"Nearly there!" said Willow, trying to be cheerful.

At long last she reached the clearing in front of the dragon's cave. Hiding behind the same rock that Godwin had leaped onto only a few days before, she tried to ignore the creeping feeling that she had done the wrong thing by coming on her own. But then she heard a faint snoring from inside the cave, and remembered why she was here.

"We're the only ones who can help. Come on, Lettuce!"

Inside the cave, it was dark, but there was a pulsing glow coming from further in. Tiptoeing carefully, Willow nearly cried out when she saw she'd almost stepped on the dragon's tail.

"This is it, Lettuce!" she whispered. The tail had vicious spines, so she stepped carefully. She followed it into the darkness. The smell grew stronger as she went, and soon she was holding her hand over her nose. Finally, she found herself staring up at an enormous sleeping dragon. Its skin was pitted with boils and pimples.

"You poor thing . . ." whispered Willow.

The dragon's flank heaved in and out as it snored, and Willow saw that the pulsing glow was caused by small balls

of flame that came from its nostrils with each breath.

As her eyes adjusted to the dim light, Willow noticed something odd. On the floor of the cave were what looked like children's toys, made from pieces of wood, clay and feathers. They had been arranged as if they

were having a tea party, and Willow realised
with horror that they looked familiar.

One had yellow feather curls on its
head, and another had black twigs sticking
straight up. The last two had red moss
for hair – one was a wild tangle, and the
other was long and wavy.

"It's us, Lettuce!" whispered Willow. "The dragon has made us into toys!"

But Lettuce didn't reply. With a gulp, Willow realised that the snoring had stopped. Slowly turning around, she looked up to see the furious face of the dragon staring down at her.

15.

THE BANK OF MILK

Boog sat back in his huge throne-like chair and burped. He put his feet up on his desk, and looked out across his new bank headquarters. Several barbarians were sitting behind makeshift booths, each with a small tap at the front. The taps were connected to long hoses, which led to to five enormous barrels.

A bedraggled queue of villagers stood in front of the booths, waiting their turn. When they came forward, each person held a small wooden bowl under the tap. The barbarian teller squirted a tiny portion of milk into it, and the villager was moved along with a curt, "NEXT."

This morning, one villager was refusing to move along. He was tall and blond, and his face was creased with disgust as he peered into his bowl.

"This isn't enough! We have all been working night and day to fill these barrels. We're exhausted and starving!"

Two barbarians wielding clubs started walking towards the man, looking delighted that they finally had something to do. Most of them had found that being a banker wasn't as fun as being a barbarian.

Boog sighed and stood up, walking towards the commotion.

"Now, now lads, I'm sure we can sort this out in a civilised manner," said Boog, holding his hands up. He pointed at the blond man. "What's your name?"

Even though the man was tall, Boog towered above him.

"My name is Gideon, and I am chief

of this village."

"Not anymore you're not!" said Oog, sticking his makeshift monocle back on his face. "You now answer to CEO Boog!"

Boog looked confused. "What's 'CEO' mean?" he whispered.

"Chieftain of Everything, Okay?" replied Oog.

Boog liked that. "Yeah, and as Chieftain of Everything, Okay, I'm telling you that we're gonna have to make an example of you. Take him away, lads!"

As quick as a flash, the two guards grabbed Gideon by his arms, and dragged him out of the bank.

"Right," said Boog, clapping his hands once. "Cancel my meetings this afternoon, Oog. I've got some cheese dreams to catch up on."

16.

NIGHT FLIGHT

Berk peered over the flying machine's basket and felt his stomach do a backflip.

Godwin was steering the rudder with one hand,

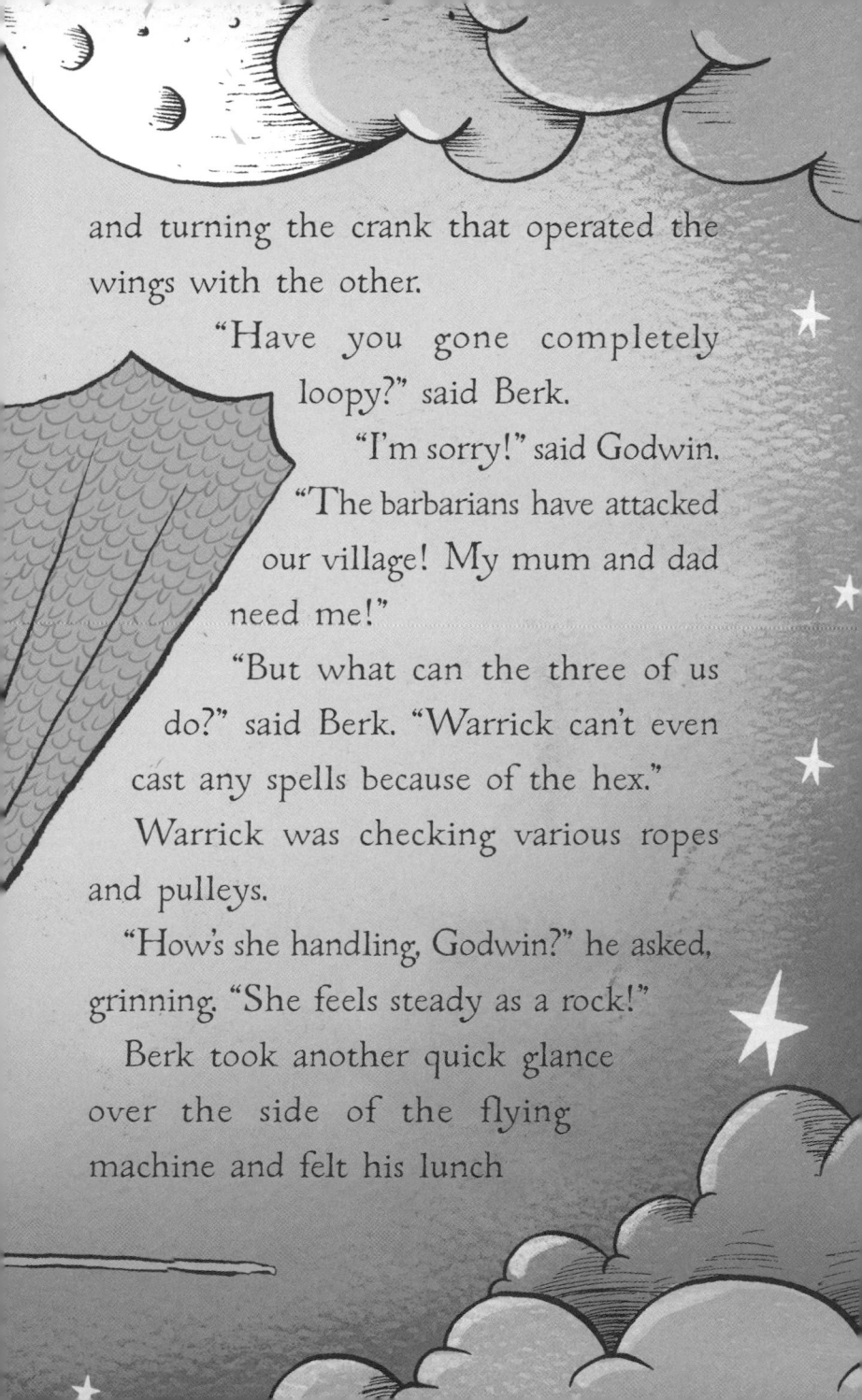

and turning the crank that operated the wings with the other.

"Have you gone completely loopy?" said Berk.

"I'm sorry!" said Godwin. "The barbarians have attacked our village! My mum and dad need me!"

"But what can the three of us do?" said Berk. "Warrick can't even cast any spells because of the hex."

Warrick was checking various ropes and pulleys.

"How's she handling, Godwin?" he asked, grinning. "She feels steady as a rock!"

Berk took another quick glance over the side of the flying machine and felt his lunch sloshing around in his tummy.

"You've *both* gone loopy. How do you even know where you're going, Godwin?"

"Our village is as far north as you can go, so I'm just following the North Star until we get to the sea."

"How do you know which one is the North Star?" asked Berk.

Warrick pointed ahead. "See that cluster of stars that looks like a saucepan? Imagine if you tipped your soup out of it – that

bright star where the soup would land is called Polaris, or the North Star."

"Stop going on about soup!" wailed Berk, and he ran to the edge of the flying machine – just in time.

Berk felt warm sun on his eyelids. He'd had a terrible dream about beating dragon's wings and rolling seas of soup.

He snapped his eyes open and saw that he was in the middle of a large, sunny field. Nearby, Warrick and Godwin were crouching behind a fallen tree.

"What happened," Berk rasped.

"You threw up a lot and then you fell

asleep," said Warrick. "Godwin and I landed the flying machine – it was a bit bumpy – and you *still* didn't wake up."

Warrick was looking through a long tube with a thick glass lens at each end. He passed it to Berk. "Look through the little end," he whispered, "down there . . ." and he pointed at a tiny village far below.

Confused, Berk put the smaller lens to his eye and peered through. He nearly dropped the spyglass – the scene in the village below suddenly seemed

much closer. "Barbarians!" he gulped.

"They've put my dad in a cage!" said Godwin. "We've got to do something!"

"Like what?" spluttered Berk. "Throw acorns at them? They look massive from far away – imagine how big they'll be up close!"

Berk looked at the flying machine, which was being gently nuzzled by a cow. Somewhere above their heads a bird squawked.

"Actually, I think I've just had an idea . . . "

17.

A Dragon of Sorts

"You want to disguise the flying machine as a dragon? They'll never fall for it!" said Godwin. "Besides, Sir Dane says that you civilise barbarians by bashing them over the head with swords. It's the knightly way!"

"That doesn't sound very chivalrous!" said Berk. "Besides, everyone knows barbarians are as thick as trolls' legs."

"I think it could work." said Warrick. "Let's rescue the village as quickly as possible so we can get home. I'm worried about Willow."

Berk stared at the flying machine. "How

on earth are we going to make this thing look like a dragon?"

Godwin clicked his fingers. "The caves on the other side of this field are full of fire beetles. There's still some of Uncle Gregory's jars in the flying machine that we used to keep nails in. We could fill them with beetles so they look like glowing eyes."

"Great idea!" said Warrick. "Let's get a fire going. I think that plant with the yellow flowers over there is called bedstraw. Mum stuffs our mattresses with it. If you boil the roots you get a bright red dye.

We can use it as paint."

"Brilliant!" said Berk. "Let's get cracking!"

"Please, let my husband go!"

Boog looked down at the woman with golden hair.

"Sorry, love, he's got to stay in his little box. We have to show what happens when you make a fuss, don't we?"

Gideon gave his wife a reassuring look from inside his cage. "Please don't worry Eleanor. I'm fine."

"See? He's fine." Boog turned to face the

rest of the villagers.

"RIGHT, ladies and gentlemen.

I'm sorry to say that you haven't listened proper. We said we wanted these barrels full by the full moon. They're not full, and it's full moon tonight. What ARE we going to do?"

Eleanor stepped forwards. "But you've been using the milk up faster than we can fill the barrels. It isn't fair!"

Boog suddenly stopped smiling. "Fair? What's FAIR got to do with anything? I was born in a puddle and ate nothing but mud until I was eleven! Was that fair?"

He pulled *Civilisation for Peasants* from the folds of his furs, and waved it around.

"The only way to make a civilised society is to be strong enough to take what you want! The Romans had the right idea!"

He looked furious, but Eleanor stood

her ground. "We didn't need the Romans here, and we don't need you either!"

"Put her in a box too!" Boog yelled at his guards. "In fact, put them ALL in boxes!"

Oog was wondering if they had enough cages for everyone, when he noticed two glowing lights in the sky.

"What's that?" he said, pointing.

Villagers and barbarians peered into the clouds as the mysterious lights grew bigger. Suddenly a piercing screech split the sky, and something red with terrible burning eyes burst out of the clouds.

Oog's monocle fell off his face and he screamed one word at the top of his voice:

18.

UNDER SIEGE

Warrick watched the barbarians and villagers scatter below them.

"It's working! More screeching, Berk!"

Berk put his lips to the horn-shaped piece of bark that protruded from the front of the flying machine and did his best dragon impression.

SkkRRAAAWWKKk!

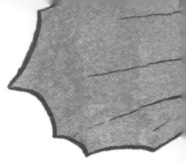

"Wow, this thing really makes me louder. Release some eggs, Warrick!"

Warrick opened a flap at the back of the flying machine. They had found a bunch of rotten eggs in an abandoned nest.

"Godwin, get me nice and low."

Oog looked up and saw the dragon sweep in an arc, then dive towards the ground.

"It's attacking!" he screamed. "Everyone take cov—"

Something exploded right in Oog's face.

SPLAT!

"It's pooing on us!" he yelled.

The barbarians started running around in a blind panic, bumping into each other and tripping over their clubs. The villagers crowded together, and several tried to break the lock on Gideon's cage.

"What a blooming shambles!" said Boog. "I'll have to deal with this myself."

He grabbed a spear from the ground and positioned himself behind a tree.

From the flying machine, Berk peered at the chaos in the village. "We've got them on the run! I reckon one more pass with some first rate screeching and

egg chucking will have
them running for the hills!"

Godwin pushed the rudder
again, and the flying machine turned.

"Get ready with the eggs, Warrick!"
yelled Berk. But before Warrick could
release his stinky payload, Boog leaped
from behind the tree, spear in hand.

"Look out!" screamed Berk.

Boog hurled the spear with all his
might. With a huge yank on the rudder,
Godwin managed to steer them out of its

path just in time, clipping Boog's shoulder and knocking him into a puddle.

"I hate puddles!" growled Boog.

Oog rushed to his boss's side. He looked at Boog's shoulder, which was streaked with red.

"You're wounded, boss!"

He put out his hand to staunch the flow of blood, and then noticed something strange. He lifted the red stuff to his fingers and sniffed it.

"Hang on, that's not blood!" Oog squinted at the dragon, which was wobbling after its sudden turn. Then he saw a small hand poking out of what looked like the dragon's bottom, dropping eggs.

"It's a trick, boss! That's no dragon!"

Boog stood up and yelled at the top of his voice.

"We've been had, lads! Let's show this fake dragon you don't mess with barbarians!"

145

19.
RUMBLED

"I think we've been rumbled!" cried Berk, ducking to avoid a rock whizzing past his ear. The flying machine was being pelted with rocks, and its wings were peppered with holes from the barbarian's missiles.

"Brace yourselves!" cried Godwin. "We're going down!"

The flying machine spiralled towards the ground at an alarming speed.

"Aim for the duckpond!" cried Godwin. All three boys grabbed onto the rudder and heaved. They landed with a splash.

※

Godwin, Berk and Warrick stared up at the huge barbarian. They were shivering with fear, and dripping with pond weed.

"Well, well, well. I don't mind telling you that you had some of the lads going for a while there!" said Boog. "Not me, obviously, but this lot were all terrified!"

The other barbarians were busy rounding up the villagers. Godwin scraped

some mud from his hair, revealing a golden curl. Gideon and Eleanor gasped.

"Godwin?"

"Mum! Dad!" sniffed Godwin. "I'm sorry!"

"Oh how heartwarming, a family reunion!" said Boog. "Well, as a little treat, you can all go in the same cage. I might be a barbarian, but I'm not a monster."

"Umm, are we not bankers anymore then, boss?" asked Oog.

"Nah, being a banker is boring!" said Boog. "Besides, I need to find some way to work off all this cheese. Nothing like a good scrap to keep you trim."

The barbarians cheered, and Boog raised his arms in reply. Godwin suddenly noticed a copy of *Civilisation for Peasants* sticking out of the barbarian's belt. But before he could say anything, there was an ear-piercing screech and, once more, everyone turned to the skies.

"Oh, more of you is there?" said Boog. "Get your rocks ready, lads!"

A dark shape appeared above them, and as the barbarians readied themselves

it grew larger and larger. All of a sudden, with a great flapping of wings and a deafening roar, a huge purple dragon landed on the ground with an earth-shaking THUD. It spread its wings, blocking out the sunlight, and reared up on its hind legs.

ROOAAARRR

"Willow!" cried Warrick. From the dragon's back, Willow gave them all a thumbs up.

"Well, I must admit – she's done a better job making her dragon than you lot did!" said Boog. "Very realistic. Shame about the funny smell though."

Boog picked up his club and strode towards the dragon.

"Err, um, boss?" said Oog, trembling. "I think . . . "

But it was too late. The dragon belched out a huge ball of flame, which engulfed Boog completely. When the smoke cleared, Boog looked a very sorry figure indeed. His clothes had been burned away, leaving him scorched and trembling in nothing but his charred underpants.

"That does it!" he yelled. "From now on we're going to be hermits! Come on, lads, let's go home!" And with that, Boog ran back up the mountain, followed by the rest of the barbarian horde.

20.

A HAPPY REUNION

"**S**top it, I'm covered in pond weed!" complained a smiling Godwin. Eleanor and Gideon were hugging him, even though he smelled like a duck's privy.

The rest of the villagers were staring up at the huge dragon.

"It's okay," Willow said. "He won't hurt you." She slid off the dragon's back and patted his side.

Berk cleared his throat.

"Ahem! Er, thanks for saving us, and s-sorry about that whole stink-bomb thing." The dragon looked down at him and snorted. Berk had the feeling he wasn't completely forgiven.

Warrick hugged his sister. "How on earth did you tame him?"

"I didn't 'tame' him. I made friends with him. He was just lonely! Not even the animals wanted anything to do with him because of the smell. He had some horrible sores, so Lettuce and I made some ointment with vinegar and herbs. He just  needed a bit of love and attention really."

Suddenly, there was

a fizzing sound, and an orb of purple light appeared in the air. A hand popped out of it, groping around blindly. It seemed to get hold of some invisible object, which it turned with a click. A door opened out of nowhere, and Wenlock, Willow and Warrick's dad, stepped out.

"There you all are!" he said, looking at the children and beaming. Patience trotted out behind him, followed by Isobel, Hildred and Gregory, who looked

a little ill. "Interdimensional travel doesn't suit this one," said Isobel. "Do you need a bucket, love?"

Later that night, everyone was gathered around a huge table in the village green. A bonfire blazed merrily as plates were piled high with food.

Berk stuffed a slice of cheese pie into

his mouth. He was very happy to see his family again. He gently nudged Patience with his elbow.

"What was that for, troll-breath?" she said.

"It's a thank you, goblin-teeth," said Berk uncomfortably. "If you hadn't been out on your horse when we flew off, Mum and Dad would have never known

where we were. We would have had to fly home on Willow's dragon, and I don't think he likes me very much!"

"He's not MY dragon!" said Willow. "And could you blame him for not liking you? It was your troll-breath stink bomb that made him so ill in the first place!"

"You can hardly smell him at all now," said Hildred. Her and Isobel had scrubbed the dragon with rose water, and dressed his wounds.

"I don't care who he belongs to," said Gideon. "He saved us from those barbarians, so he's welcome in this village."

"I've been thinking about that," said Gregory. "Why doesn't he stay here with you, brother? Those barbarians wouldn't dare come back with him here. He can hold the fort until Godwin becomes a knight. What do you think, Willow?"

"It's a great idea!" she said. "He would rather stay here than have to go back to that miserable old cave."

Eleanor brushed a tear from her eye. "You've all done so much for us! The cow pump that Warrick invented is going to save us so much time."

Warrick had adapted his chicken-feather pump to help milk the cows, and had spent the afternoon showing the villagers how to use it.

"Taming dragons, milking cows,

vanquishing bullies. It's what we good knights do!" said Godwin.

Berk looked awkward for a moment. "Erm, so I know it might seem that I can be a bit, well, mean to you sometimes, Godwin, but I'm not, well . . . erm, what I mean is . . . erm."

Patience interrupted. "What he actually thinks is that you're the best cousin ever and he

wishes he could be more like you."

"Shut UP, witch-nose!" said Berk.

"There's one bully we still need to vanquish though," said Warrick.

Godwin remembered the copy of *Civilisation for Peasants* he had seen sticking out of Boog's robes and stared angrily into the fire.

"Sir Dane . . . " he growled.

21.

THE DOWNFALL OF SIR DANE

"Settle down, fauntkins. I trust you all had a restful weekend?"

Berk, Willow, Godwin and Warrick all looked nervously at each other. They were gathered on the school field, sitting on the ground with the rest of the class for Sir Dane's swordsmanship lesson. Today Sir Dane was grinning more than usual and he had a nasty glint in his eyes.

"I feel certain that most of you will be relieved to hear that I have solved the mystery of the missing tapestries."

Berk's blood instantly turned to ice, but he tried as hard as he could to keep his expression as normal as possible.

"I had Percival the groundskeeper drain the moat, and there they were, tied to a rock. They were in a terrible mess. It almost looked like someone had used them to mop up a privy."

At this he smiled coldly, and cast a chilling look at Berk, Willow and Warrick. "For today's lesson, I have devised a simple test to divide the plebeians from the upper crust once and for all. I think we'll start with you. Stand up!

He pointed a finger at Warrick.

"How are we meant to strike fear and respect into the hearts of our enemies when we have hair as fluffy as a poodle's back end?"

Sir Dane made Warrick turn around slowly in front of the whole class. "It is specimens like this who will never reach the ranks of knighthood."

With that, Sir Dane drew his sword from its scabbard and thrust it into a nearby tree trunk.

"Prove me wrong, boy," said Sir Dane with a sly grin at Warrick. "Draw the sword from the trunk to regain your honour. Or do you have the heart of a chicken?"

There were several chickens from Farmer Stuffcock's barn sitting in a nearby bush, and they clucked indignantly.

Warrick looked at the sword quivering in the trunk. It was taller than he was. Luckily he knew something that Sir Dane didn't . . .

As Warrick heaved and puffed trying to get the sword out, and Sir Dane looked on with a cruel smile, Berk pulled a small straw from his pocket. He and Warrick

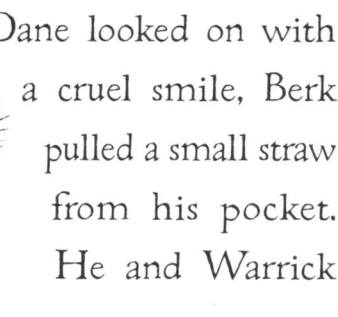

had made it from the reeds. Slowly he extended it until it reached the opening of Sir Dane's boot.

"Okay, Willow, do it!" he hissed.

Willow produced a jar from her dress, which was full of fire beetles. She carefully tipped them into the hollow of the straw.

Godwin, Berk and Willow watched Sir Dane without breathing. He was pointing and jeering at Warrick, who was still pretending to try and heave the sword out of the trunk.

Suddenly Sir Dane leaped into the air, and began spasming wildly. "Gadzooks!" he yelled. "My legs are on fire!"

The whole class stared in disbelief at Sir Dane as he hopped about squealing and desperately scratching at his leg. Godwin stuck his foot out and tripped up Sir Dane, who rolled across the grass and landed in the moat with a splash. After a couple of seconds he resurfaced, and with an effort pulled himself out of the water. He was completely covered in slime.

From somewhere high in the clouds there was a distant flap of wings, and, as if from nowhere, hundreds of feathers fell from the sky and covered Sir Dane from head to toe. The whole class erupted in laughter. Several of Farmer Stuffcock's chickens leaped onto

Sir Dane's shoulders and began
nuzzling him affectionately.

"Who's the chicken now, sir?" said Warrick.

Godwin shook his head in mock
disappointment.

"How uncivilised," he said, and tore his copy of *Civilisation for Peasants* in two.

Berk and Willow looked up to the sky, where the distant silhouette of a dragon gripping an empty sack disappeared into the clouds, heading north.

The End

Glossary

Some words from the medieval times are different from words today and no one uses them now . . . maybe they should?

1. Peasants – MEDIEVAL FARM LABOURERS

2. Hoddypeak – A FOOL

3. Daub – A MIXTURE OF MUD, CLAY, ANIMAL DUNG AND STRAW USED IN THE BUILDING OF HOUSES

4. Fopdoodle – ANOTHER WORD FOR FOOL

5. Mubblefubbles – DOWN IN THE DUMPS

6. Zooks or gadzooks – A MILD EXCLAMATION. IT'S A BIT LIKE SAYING 'GOODNESS ME' OR 'OH MY!'

7. Woad – A PLANT WHICH CAN BE TURNED INTO BLUE DYE. CELTIC TRIBES IN BRITAIN MAY HAVE USED IT AS WAR PAINT

8. Apothecary – A PERSON WHO MADE MEDICINES

9. Prithee — PLEASE

10. Fauntkins — CHILDREN

11. Privy — A MEDIEVAL TOILET

12. Plebian — IN ANCIENT ROME, A PERSON WITHOUT WEALTH OR STATUS

13. Flux — WHAT HAPPENED IN THE MIDDLE AGES WHEN YOU HAD AN UPSET STOMACH

14. Brangling — ARGUING OR SQUABBLING

THE INVENTOR WHOSE BOOK WARRICK READS IS BASED ON THE FAMOUS ITALIAN ARTIST AND SCIENTIST, LEONARDO DA VINCI WHO LIVED 1452–1519. LEONARDO LOOKED AT BIRDS AND BATS, AND TRIED TO WORK OUT HOW THEY FLEW. HE LEFT BEHIND SEVERAL DESIGNS FOR FLYING MACHINES, ALTHOUGH THEY WOULD NOT HAVE FLOWN.

Also available:

ISBN: 978-1-78370-812-3

Read Tom Knight's first armour-
rattling adventure in the Good Knight,
Bad Knight series.